Losing Addison

Live the Nightmare

A NOVELLA

by Marty Beaudet

CREATESPACE

This is a work of fiction. Names, characters, and
incidents are the products of the author's imagination
or are used fictitiously. Any resemblance to actual events,
persons, living or dead, is entirely coincidental.

Published in the United States.

www.losingaddison.wordpress.com

Preface

This is a true story. I'm calling it fiction because I can't trust myself to tell it accurately. I'm too close to the people and events herein to be objective. I may have changed some of the names to protect, well, perhaps myself. I can't be sure. If there are errors or omissions, they're certainly mine. And they're probably intentional.

Prologue

I'M PEERING OVER THE EDGE OF THE BED. This, I immediately realize, is a mistake. My head begins to swim at the sight of the black and white checkerboard pattern on the hospital floor. Quickly I resume my previous position, staring at the water—or is it blood—stains on the ceiling. A rusty pool of discoloration hangs directly over my head. *The House That Dripped Blood* comes to mind.

Something isn't right. I feel thick. I want to recall what happened, how I came to be here, but my thoughts won't congeal. Instead they flow in random rivulets of recollections: Kristie, my childhood home, church friends from years ago, my seventh-grade science teacher. My mother. Addison. Suddenly panic grips me. I don't know why, but my heart begins to race. And then my thoughts flow onward, beyond my control.

I'm hauled back to here and now by a knock on the open door, followed by the entry of two men in white coats. One carries a clipboard. "Lester McCubbin," he says, reciting my name under his breath as he scans what is no doubt my medical chart.

The other man speaks directly to me. "I'm Doctor Tomlinson, Lester. This is Doctor Yeats. How are you doing today?"

"Les," I correct him. No one but my mother ever calls me Lester. My father, right up until his death, only called me "son." Apparently my name was not worth remembering. I have to give him credit for acknowledging the relationship, at least. (Poor Addison was always just "boy" or, more frequently, "*the* boy," as though my father could not admit that he had sired such a disgrace.) Les was the nickname I gave myself. It summed me up quite well. Less handsome. Less popular. Less likely to succeed. It had been an easy moniker to live up to.

"What am I doing here?" I manage to ask the doctor through the thickness.

"Looks like you banged yourself up pretty good," Tomlinson says in a patronizing, first-grade classroom voice.

He pulls back the bedcovers from my right side. I'm wearing a cast from the knee down. *What the...?* How did I not notice this sooner?

"Are you in pain?" Tomlinson inquires.

I just stare at the cast, still not able to believe that it's my leg inside it.

"I take that as a 'no,'" the doctor continues, unfazed by my lack of response. Yeats scribbles. "How about your head?"

"My head?" I say, looking away from the cast at last. Reflexively I raise a hand to check my head which, for what I can tell at the moment, could be completely missing. "Jesus!" I scream, wincing at the pain and withdrawing my hand from the bandage that swaddles my head. "What the hell?"

"Two more cc's," Tomlinson says to Yeats, who nods and scribbles on his clipboard before ringing the call button.

"We'll get that taken care of," Tomlinson coos in soothing tones. "Then you can get some rest." He turns to leave, as does his toady.

Aroused by the burst of pain, I finally find my voice. "Wait!" Both men stop and regard me with concern that until now has seemed absent. "Will someone please tell me what's going on here?" It's more of a command than a question. I'm surprised at my own vehemence.

"You've had an accident," Yeats says, curtly, scolding. "We'll talk about it after you've rested some."

"Where's Addison?" My tone is suddenly plaintive. A hole has just opened up inside me. I need my brother. He would know what to do. Or at least he wouldn't stop trying until something worked.

Tomlinson regards Yeats with a look that speaks volumes, illegible to me. Yeats whispers something to Tomlinson, who nods his agreement. Yeats writes something on the clipboard. "You must try not to think about Addison right now, Lester."

I want to slug the patronizing bastard. My thoughts of revenge are interrupted by the arrival of the nurse.

Five minutes later, the needle withdrawn from my arm, I'm losing consciousness. *Addison. Addison. Addison.* Am I saying this or just thinking it?

Chapter 1

HE'S EVERYTHING I'M NOT: tall, blond, athletic, outgoing. He's got a devil-may-care attitude toward life that's always getting him into trouble. It seems I've spent most of my life apologizing for him and taking the blame for his misadventures while he was already off to the next one. I guess that comes with being a twin.

We're the fraternal kind, not identical. Still, that never kept people from confusing us for one another. Despite our disparate appearances, he was often called Les, and I, Addison. If he did something wrong, I often got punished. It never seemed the other way around. Yet when he accomplished something of merit, he still got the praise. At least from my mother.

My mother always enjoyed Addison's company, despite his propensity for acting out. My father felt differently. Once when I was about ten, I heard my parents arguing. Mom called Addison "special" and "gifted"; Dad said he was "loony" and "dangerous" and should be locked up. Mom got really angry then. Angrier than I'd ever seen her, before or since. She told my Dad she'd rather see him locked up.

That moment always stuck with me. I couldn't understand why Addison angered my father so, and yet pleased my mother just as much. Whatever the reason, I often felt invisible. I never heard them fight about me that way. I sensed that my father was disappointed in me, however. The recognition I got from him was sporadic and halfhearted at best. He went through the motions of parenting, but it felt like a chore. He patted me on the back from time to time, but it always seemed to be accompanied by a sigh of resignation that I was never going to amount to much.

Addison, on the other hand, provoked my father frequently. While I got an occasional spanking, Addison was close to beaten. If not for my mother's intervention, he probably would have been. I can still see clearly the veins in my father's neck, the rush of blood to his face, the craziness in his eyes. At times I wished that I could be worthy of all that. Anything to prove that I existed, that someone could feel passionately about me, even if only in anger. Eventually however, I grew to embrace my solitude. Apart from Addison, that is.

They say twins share a special bond. That has certainly been my experience. Addison and I are usually aware of each other's thoughts before either of us speaks them. This isn't as cool as it sounds though. In fact, it's been more of a curse than a blessing. For me anyway. Addison doesn't seem to care one way or the other. He just shrugs off whatever displeases him. And when my thoughts get too intrusive for him, he just walks away. Leaves. Who knows where he goes. But wherever it is, it's far enough that we can't hear each other anymore.

These breaks are a relief for me. People often think that because Addison and I are twins we must think alike. But that's not true. We disagree a lot. I mean a whole bunch. And we often fight about it, sometimes openly, but more often just between ourselves. Whatever discretion we exercise is usually my doing, because when our fights become public, he usually disappears and I'm left to bear the consequences.

Like the time I was in the U.S. Coast Guard, stationed at Ramey Air Force Base in Puerto Rico, and Addison came to visit me.

Chapter 2

"**Hey, Bro!**" **Addison's arrival** was out of the blue, as always.

"Dude, what are you doing here? You're not supposed to be in here," I said. "How'd you get past security?" I don't know why I bothered asking. Addison never revealed his secrets.

"Not to worry," he replied, cheerfully sidestepping the question. "I'm here to spring you."

"Uh-uh, not this time," I demurred. "I'm on KP in two hours. Gonna have to take a rain check."

"No sweat, dude. We'll be back in time."

I don't remember the details of the conversation, but Addison prevailed, as he always did. He always gets his way. That's the downside of reading each other's thoughts. He's stronger than I am.

To be fair, it wasn't entirely his fault. I hadn't seen Addison in nearly eighteen months—the longest period we'd ever been apart. I guess that's why I gave in. I wanted to go to Rincon Beach with him a lot more than I wanted to work KP.

Rincon is a famous surfers' beach on the island of Puerto Rico. It was only thirty minutes from the base, so it was theoretically possible to get there and back in two hours. There were two problems, however. Neither Addison nor I had a car. And I wasn't cleared to leave the installation. Not that we let that stop us. We hitch-hiked from the gate on the main highway, and got there just forty-five minutes later.

Just watching the awesome breakers and hearing their alternating susurrant and explosive rhythms was enough to make me happy. But Addison wanted more. He always wants more. He was determined to go body surfing, not caring a whit about the signs that said: *Aviso. ¡Peligro! Riptide. Es prohibido bañarse.* I tried to dissuade him, pleading both his case—the danger—as well as my own—the time needed to return to the base. But, to paraphrase Ray Stevens: it was too late—I'd already been mooned.

I kicked off my shoes and ran after him, closing in just as he splashed into the receding tidewater. We both went down, me, fully clothed, Addison, butt naked. Salt, sand, and sadness washed over me, into my eyes and nose and mouth. I hate fighting with my brother.

Addison cursed. I spit and flailed and screamed. Not at him, but at the pain in the big toe on my right foot. Upon inspection of the blood- and salt-drenched wound there I discovered that a piece of coral had lodged itself under my toenail.

Addison only laughed. "That's what you get for breaking the rules, Bro." That's when I screamed at him. Not that it did any good. He was already hightailing it back to the highway.

It took us nearly half an hour—spent entirely in silence—to get a ride back to the base. The driver stopped about a quarter-mile short of the main gate, not wanting to invite any inquiries from the guards on duty. They kind of had a thing for picking on the locals who came poking around.

I hopped out gingerly and began limping toward the gate. Addison stayed in the back of the truck, however. I didn't see him again for another six months—the week I was given a medical discharge from the Coast Guard because of an uncontrolled infection in my right leg.

Chapter 3

"You're a sucker and a fool."

"Thanks for the encouragement," I deadpanned. We were both in our second year in college at Utah State. I had just announced my engagement. I can't say I expected any better response from my brother.

"I mean, really," Addison said with a sneer. "You expect me to believe that you're going to settle down with two-point-three children and a wife, and live happily ever after?"

"It could happen." My response was hardly a resounding vote of confidence in the decision I'd made. Already he was undermining my intentions.

Addison laughed uproariously. "I can see it now. You'll run screaming at the first dirty diaper." He laughed again.

"Aw, c'mon," I pleaded. "Would you lay off for once?"

"Yeah, right. Whatever," he said with his usual nonchalance. "Lemme tell you about my last date."

I rolled my eyes. I didn't want to hear it, but it was useless to try to stop him.

"This guy in my Chinese class, Rick? Well, we both showed up to apply for the same job the other day. Something on campus called 'Stores'—I'm not really sure what all it involves. Anyway, we got to talking. I think he likes me."

"You think every guy likes you," I said, unable to resist the jab. "Right up until you meet his wife or girlfriend."

"Shut the fuck up, Bro," Addison said without real animosity. "You're hardly one to be giving out relationship advice."

"Maybe so," I said. "But I'm entitled. The last time you messed around with a guy, I was the one who ended up with his wife crying on my shoulder. You ought to at least stray farther from home when you choose your victims."

"Can't," he said, without compunction. "We know all the same people." He threw an Aerobie football at me from the couch. "But, hey, speaking of straying from home. Rick's driving to Vegas this weekend. He's invited us to tag along."

"Both of us? I don't even know the guy."

"Yeah, but I told him all about you. I told him we were inseparable, and he invited you too."

"Why would you do that? Isn't this supposed to be a hot date?"

"I dunno," he shrugged. "Could be. I just wasn't sure where he was coming from and I didn't want to seem too forward."

"Jesus, you're an idiot."

"Hey, runs in the family, I hear," he said, flashing me the impish grin that has always been both boon and bane to me for as long as I can remember.

"Well, I'm busy this weekend. Kristie's leaving for her Peace Corps tour in two weeks and I—

Addison cut me off. "I already told him we'd go."

"Well, just tell him I can't!" I was getting irritated now.

"C'mon, Les. I need you. That's a long ride with someone I hardly know. It might not work out."

"You should've thought of that before you agreed to it." As usual, he'd put me in the parental role to his unfettered inner child.

"Hey, we could visit Gene!" he said with an enthusiasm that completely disregarded my objections. "Remember, that guy from the track team back at Westdale?"

"Oh, right. We haven't seen him since high school. Like we're just going to show up and say, 'Hey, remember us?'"

"Aw, c'mon. He was an awesome dude. It'll be fun."

Chapter 4

VEGAS WAS A DISASTER. Gene was nice enough, but we spent far too long engaged in awkward pleasantries. Addison had abandoned me on Gene's doorstep, so I had no way of escaping the awkwardness until Addison and Rick came back for me.

For all of Gene's "awesomeness" in Addison's memory, once we got there my brother decided that things were "going to work" with Rick after all, and they quickly withdrew to a cheap motel room. Meanwhile, Gene and I reminisced about how little we had in common.

A Mormon, Gene was married with three kids already. I was barely engaged to a girl who was about to leave the country for a year. "Wow," Gene said. "Sounds like somebody's a little commitment-phobic!"

He meant it to be humorous, but it was true. I had gotten engaged using the ROTC model: pledge now, serve later. I really just liked saying I was engaged because it sounded like I was becoming a responsible adult. I knew I wasn't ready, but I was hoping the engagement would force me to become ready.

It was in the third tedious hour of comparing Gene's accomplishments with my lack of them that my cell rang. It was Addison. "Hey, Bro," he slurred. "Jid joo know that dreeks are free in the casino? Godda be gabblin' though."

"Addison!" I barked, while trying not to let Gene hear what was up. "Where are you? You were supposed to pick me up an hour ago."

"Can't, Bro. We're druck. Godda call a cab."

I switched off the phone. I wasn't sure if he meant me or himself, but there was no point in having any further conversation. I needed to call a cab.

I took my leave of Gene and returned to the motel. The room was empty, but one of the two beds looked like a tornado had hit it. For a moment I considered just throwing myself on the other one and shutting out the world, I was so angry. But my unrelenting sense of responsibility took over, as it always did where Addison was concerned. I needed to make sure he was all right. Somebody had to look after him, if he wouldn't do it for himself.

I hit my phone's redial to connect with the last incoming number. Addison didn't answer. He knew I'd be pissed and was likely screening calls. Rick's car was in the lot, which meant either that they were nearby, or they'd cabbed down to the Strip. If it was the latter, I had no hope of finding them. I walked six blocks to the nearest dump of a casino, hoping they'd kept their mischief close to home.

No such luck. I sat down to ponder my next move. *Fuck 'em!* Rick and Addison were both adults, I decided. They could take care of themselves. I had nearly convinced myself of this when a fifty-something barmaid in a twenty-something miniskirt wobbled up on four-inch stilettos and offered to take my drink order. I happened to be sitting in front of a nickel slot that she obviously thought I intended to play.

I wasn't a gambler. Nor did I drink. Until that moment. *Fuck 'em!* I told myself again. I didn't owe anybody anything. I was an adult too. I had just as much right to cut loose as anybody. I ordered a rum and coke. It had been the drink of choice back in Puerto Rico, where the locally produced rum was cheap. What I didn't realize until many years later was that it was also a deadly mix of caffeine and alcohol. After my third—or was it fourth?—free drink I was out of nickels, and anything else that could be converted to nickels. *Shit.*

So much for "cutting loose." I was drunk and horny and broke. Not a good combination. Depression began to set in as I stumbled back to the motel. I hadn't gone a block when a full-figured platinum-blonde in a Tina Turner get-up accosted me. "Hey, honey," she growled. "You look like you could use some help." She reached a thick arm out to steady me. "What's your name?"

"Lesh," I slurred.

She guffawed in a disconcertingly deep, hoarse voice. Clearly a smoker. "Lush? Well you got me convinced!" She laughed again.

I didn't bother to correct her.

Just then a familiar voice rang out. "Hey, Bro!" Addison was approaching from the motel. Either he had sobered up since I last spoke to him, or I was so drunk it only seemed so.

"Who's your friend?" he asked as he reached the corner on which I was barely standing. "Hey, I'm Addison," he said to the woman without waiting for my reply.

"Hi. I'm Tina." She offered Addison her hand, palm down, wrist limp. Even in my rum-induced haze I cringed when he kissed it.

"You jont know where that handj been," I scolded. Addison exploded in a fit of laughter, while "Tina" pulled back in what I'm sure now was mock indignation.

"Honey, it's not where it's been that matters. It's where it can be," she said, grabbing my ass in her vice-like claw.

"Can't," I said, despite my obvious state of arousal. "Too druck. Beshides, I'm broke too."

"No worries, Bro!" Addison crowed. "Rick and I hit the jackpot down at the Luxor!" He shoved a wad of bills toward me.

I just stared at them, not sure what to make of the development. I was starting to get dizzy and just wanted to get back to the motel.

"Well, take it, Honey," Tina advised me, reaching toward Addison's outstretched hand and pushing it closer to me. "Don't look a gift horse in the..."

Her words were cut short by a brief, sharp siren burst and a cop car screeching to a stop on the curb beside us. I threw up.

Chapter 5

"**LADY WAS A DUDE.**" Those were the first words I heard out of Addison's mouth after I woke up in the holding cell the next morning. Apparently I'd passed out right after puking.

"What's going on?" I could see we were in jail, but I was still fuzzy on the details.

"The whore you tried to pick up was a dude, Bro."

Fuck. I didn't know which was worse: that I'd been arrested, or that I'd been too stupid to know a guy from a girl. "I wasn't trying to pick her...uh...*him*...whatever. I wasn't picking anybody up!"

"Not what the cops say. They've got the cash to prove it. *My* winnings, I might add." Addison's own incarceration hadn't dampened his spirits any. He started to sing: *L-O-L-A, Lo-la...*

"Shut the fuck up!" I screamed. My voice was hoarse, no doubt from repeated puking. My brother's rendition of the Kinks' song became a hum, but did not cease.

Despite Addison's cajoling, the police did not let him use his gambling profits to post our $500 bail. They were holding it as evidence. He called Rick. There was no answer. The desk clerk at the motel said Rick had checked out before 8 AM. Hightailing it back to Utah, no doubt.

Couldn't say I blamed him. Who'd want to be tangled up with a couple of fuck-ups like us? Prostitution. *Shit.* I didn't dare call anyone I knew, even to bail me out. How would I explain?

"Call that pastor dude who's always giving you such great advice," Addison said, his tone mocking.

"Oh, right." My head ached at the thought of having such a conversation.

"No, I mean it. He's always telling you how much he wants to help you. This'd be a *huge* help, Bro."

"No way," I protested. "Just drop it."

"Got any better ideas?"

"Just let me think, OK?"

Addison got up and went to the cell bars. "Guard? Hey! Yo!"

A surly uniform appeared in nothing resembling a hurry.

"Dude. Can I get another phone call?" Addison inquired.

"Wait," I said, jumping to my feet. "Who are you going to call?"

The guard was already unlocking the door.

"Chill, Bro. I got this covered."

The charges were eventually dropped, but not until we'd spent four days in Nevada, followed by another day on the road back to Logan. We'd missed three entire days of classes, but that wasn't the worst of it. Addison had called Pastor Bateman, director of the campus Christian Center, in spite of my adamancy to the contrary.

Bateman had not only wired the bail money; his helpfulness extended to excusing our absence to the professors whose classes we'd missed. The story of our humiliating "crime"—never mind the dropped charges— was all over campus by the time we got back. It was only a matter of days before we were hauled before the Scholarship Committee on whose dime we had been enrolled at the university.

We were both expelled for "conduct unbecoming." Well, not expelled exactly, but our scholarships were rescinded, leaving us no course but to withdraw at the end of the semester. Even if I'd had the money I was too mortified to stay at the school. I was more than ready to hop the next bus out of town by the time the term ended.

Addison was, as usual, eager for a new adventure. He was headed for sunny California. I couldn't think of any reason not join him. We rented a U-Haul trailer, slapped it onto our Mustang, and headed west.

Chapter 6

IT'S HARD TO TELL HOW LONG I've been in this hospital. For one thing, the drug-induced bouts of sleep are so deep they resemble unconsciousness. And I have no clue how long they last. Then there's the complete absence of natural light in the room, so that I have no sense of day and night. There is no television and no clock. I was apparently stripped of my watch and cell phone upon my arrival, as I haven't seen either of them since waking up here on the first day. Or was it night?

I had thought that the gauzy curtain on the wall to my right covered a window; that the simple raising of a blind would let some much-desired sunlight in. But when I asked Michael, one of the nurses, to open it, he shook his head. "Ain't no sunshine in here, sunshine," he said in a lazy drawl. (And why are all the nurses male here?) Later, when a PT nurse brushed the curtain aside for a moment, I saw that it concealed a two-way mirror. Or is it a one-way window? Anyway, I'm sure it's the kind that can be seen through only from the other side. At times I can sense just a hint of movement beyond it. At least, I think I can. And I get the feeling that someone is watching me. It must be the nurses' station. Still, it's creepy.

I'm normally claustrophobic. That my confinement here hasn't driven me crazy yet is probably due to the constant meds. I still don't know what they are or what they're for exactly, except pain. I don't think I need so much medication now, though. I'm finally able to touch the bandage on my head without recoiling, even when the painkillers are at an ebb. I'm going to ask the doctor to lower the dosage.

"Good news, Mr. McCubbin," says Michael, who suddenly fills my doorframe. (All the nurses refuse to call me Les.) "Doctor gonna remove y'all's stitches today. Then you be ready to move to a recovery room."

"I didn't know I had any," I say without inflection. I'm ambivalent about this development.

Ignoring my declaration of ignorance, Michael continues his cheerleading routine. "Ain't that good news?" His goofy grin assures me that it is.

I have to admit that, in spite of my persistent frustration over the lack of information I'm given, and a complete cluelessness about where I am to begin with, the idea of leaving this room for any other destination does give rise to a subdued excitement in me.

As promised, with the stitches and bandage now gone from my head, I'm being wheeled to a "recovery room." Michael, whose full 350 pounds of biomass is propelling me just a touch too enthusiastically down a heavily chlorinated, mint-walled corridor, has not stopped extolling the virtues of my new digs since our journey began five minutes earlier.

"Ain't none too big, mind you, but y'all are gonna have a real window. And they won't be none of them beepin' machines to keep you 'wake, like they do."

"Sounds lovely," I say without conviction. I wonder, not for the first time, if I've been lobotomized. I keep thinking I should feel more than I do. More anger. More vehemence about demanding answers. More longing for Addison, about whom I still have been told nothing.

We arrive at Room 301-B. The door is already open. Michael

wheels me inside and stops. "Well? Ain't it every bit as nice as I told y'all?"

He was right about the size. I'm estimating it's about ten by twelve. There's a frameless twin bed under the window, no bigger than the bed I just left, but without all the hospital trappings. Beside the bed is an orange fabric-wrapped cube upon which sits a paperback copy of "The Good News." *Yeah, right.* I tell myself sardonically. I could use some real good news about now.

"Well, go on," Michael cajoles. "Git y'all's ass outta this chair. You don't need it no more."

This news catches me off guard. I haven't had control over my own mobility for so long, it takes me a few seconds to remember how. I stand up tentatively. "Uh, what about this?" I ask Michael, pointing at the cast on my leg. I have just now remembered it myself.

Michael's a step ahead of me. He's already grabbed a pair of crutches that were leaning against the wall by the door. I take them and try them out. It feels strange to walk again. I'm not too steady. Michael beams anyway. "Y'all are gonna be real comfortable here," he assures me, as though I'm checking into a hotel.

My thoughts turn to the overarching benefit the room offers me: sunlight. I hobble over to the window and pull aside the heavy, blackout curtain. "*Rejas?*" I say, recalling the word from my days in Puerto Rico. I'm referring to the iron bars that shroud the wire-infused, nonshatter glass. In Puerto Rico these are on the outside of the window. Here they are on the inside. "What's with—" I begin, turning to ask Michael.

Still smiling, Michael has already backed out of the room with the wheelchair and is closing the door.

"Hey, wait!" I hobble across the ten or twelve feet of indoor-outdoor carpet as quickly as I can but the door has closed. I pull the handle. The door doesn't budge. It's locked from the outside.

"No no no no no!" I begin to scream. The claustrophobia is already kicking in.

Chapter 7

CALIFORNIA WAS NOT A PARTICULARLY HAPPY PLACE for me and my brother, despite the famous sunshine. It was the first time in my life I'd seen Addison discouraged about anything. Relatively, anyway. His occasional moping and lack of initiative was about equivalent to my usual condition. Even on his worst days he was nowhere near my occasional bouts of depression.

Still, the California Dreamin' we'd heard so much about turned out to be just that. Good-paying jobs were hard to come by. We both found work at an LAX airport hotel, Addison as a room-service waiter; me as a gardener, maintaining the landscaping on a crew of five. The wages covered our rent in a tiny Silverlake basement apartment, and we each got at least one meal free during our work shifts, but there wasn't much left over for entertainment.

I could only assume that all the nights Addison spent away from home were paid for by a "date." I didn't ask—and didn't particularly want to know—if there was any additional "income" involved in such transactions. After my Las Vegas experience, I wasn't even willing to have that conversation.

It was only six months later that Addison announced that he was moving out.

"C'mon, Addy," I pleaded. "It'll kill me to pay the rent by myself."

"Get a roommate," he said without obvious concern for my

predicament.

"Oh, right. Look at this place. It's barely big enough for brothers, let alone strangers."

"What about that girl you work with—what's her name, Noreen? She'd be fun, right?"

"Fun? I'm not looking for a lay. Besides, she just got engaged."

Addison just shrugged and continued gulping orange juice from the carton.

"Isn't it a little soon to be moving in with this guy anyway?" I probed. "You've known him, what, three weeks?"

"But he really, really wants me!" Addison said in a mock Broadway-musical voice.

I still saw Addison fairly often over the ensuing months, but our time together became increasingly brief as his relationship consumed him. By the end of the year, we were lucky to have more than a brief conversation a couple times a month, and never did anything together anymore. It was about that time that I decided to find a church to attend. I was horrible at meeting people, even for friendship, let alone dating. Unaccustomed to my brother's prolonged absence I had become lonely and depressed. The next five years were a new chapter in my life—the longest period to-date that Addison and I remained apart.

Shortly past the one-year mark in his relationship it ended in violence. I was both relieved and profoundly hurt that he did not turn to me at that time. It was uncharacteristic, to be sure. I knew he was hurting. We always knew these things. I could only conclude that he was either offended by my newfound religious activities or was afraid that they would cause me to scold or reject him. I held myself responsible for not reaching out to him. I shouldn't have waited for him to come to me.

Instead, he moved to San Francisco, 500 miles to the north. Neither of us could afford to travel. And neither of us was much of a writer, even with email. So our relationship subsisted on the occasional phone call, wherein he shared his latest sexual exploits and I shared my latest church news. Neither of us was very interested in the other's "lifestyle," so the calls were always brief and stilted.

It was a strange period in both our lives. Years later we would both say, "What the hell was I thinking?" about how we spent those years. The catalyst that ended that estrangement was most probably my giving up on religion. The people I'd met at church were truly kind and generous. And I'd established what I had thought were enduring friendships with four or five of them. I'd even dated a couple of the girls in the congregation and had a great time doing so. But I always balked when it came to the "commitment" stage. Without fail, each one of them eventually took me aside for "the talk." *Where is this going? What do you want out of this relationship? Don't you want kids?*

I finally walked—or as they said, *ran*—away. From the girls, the friends, and the church. My job was unsatisfying, and even the constant LA sun became an annoyance. I craved weather that more closely matched my mood: cloudy with occasional sunbreaks. Naturally I fled northward to—where else? Addison. It was then that I knew our fates were inextricably linked. We were simply unable to live complete lives without each other, in spite of the frustrations our togetherness always caused me.

Chapter 8

I'M SPENT. I HAVE NO MORE TEARS. No more screams. Only the aching void within. The place where Addison once was.

I lie in a fetal ball in a sea of orange plaid on the bed, rocking to the rhythm of my heartbeat. The room is quiet as death. I have only just now noticed the mirror. I wonder who is on the other side watching me now. I wonder what they see? A broken man? An imbecile? Les become lesser?

I can have these thoughts now because the meds have stopped. There have been no shots, no pills, and no IV drips since I've been here—which I estimate to be at least eight hours, due to the waning light through the barred window. In fact, I've not seen or heard another soul, with the exception of the arrival of a dinner tray through a receptacle in the door a few hours ago.

The returning lucidity is as much curse as blessing. Gone is the thickness that clouded my thoughts for the last, what—week? Two weeks? Gone too is the near perpetual sleep. I am wide awake now and it hurts. Not my body, but my mind. It is exhausted. I want the meds again. I've decided I prefer the thickness.

The lock turns and I start. Human contact? The door opens. It is Michael, accompanied by a doctor I've not seen before.

"Good evening, Lester."

I don't bother to tell him I'm Les.

"I'm Doctor Hunter," he says, walking toward the bed with a placid smile.

And I'm the hunted, I think about answering. Instead, I sit up on the bed and hold my tongue. I make a mental note that the return of sarcasm to my repertoire is a sign that I'm becoming myself again.

Michael doesn't enter. He says nothing and watches the doctor. Hunter turns and gives him a nod. Michael closes the door and I hear the key turn in the lock.

"How are you feeling?" the doctor asks, seating himself in the boxy yellow foam chair to my left. "Do you have any pain?"

"No," I say in a voice barely audible to myself. I clear my throat and try again. "Not physical pain."

"That's good," Hunter says. "Can you tell me what kind of pain you *do* have?"

His patronizing tone angers me, but I'm too polite to say so. "Oh, you know, inside." I don't really want to talk about it, but I fear that if I don't give him something, I'll be left alone again and the claustrophobia will consume me.

"Can you describe it to me?"

This is sounding familiar. "Are you a shrink?" I ask without preamble.

"I'm a doctor, Lester."

"Les," I correct. If we're going to be spending any amount of time together, I figure he ought to know who I am.

"Alright. *Les.*"

"Why am I locked up here? Why are there people watching me?" I point an accusing finger at the all-seeing mirror opposite his chair.

"It's for your protection."

"My protection?! It's you people I need to be protected from! Why in God's name w—" My breath catches. I've just realized what the hell is up. "Oh, fuck. I'm on suicide watch."

Hunter smiles pathetically. "You did try to harm yourself, Les."

"I didn't!" A burst of memory flares across my consciousness. Addison. Anger. Fear. "It— It— It was a fight!"

"With whom?"

"Addison!"

The doctor crosses his legs and settles deeper into the chair. "And where is Addison now?"

"I don't know." My voice quavers and I drop my gaze to my lap as the fear floods in again. "But I miss him. I need him." I look back at Hunter. "Where is he?"

"Do you remember the last time you saw him?" the doctor asks, avoiding my question.

"Yes. I mean, no." The images are coming faster now. I don't want to look at them, but I do. Tears well in my eyes and begin to spill. "I—" The words fail. I shut out the images. There's blood. So much blood.

The doctor says nothing while I sob. Minutes pass as I try to regain my composure. My sanity. Hunter waits until the heaving in my chest begins to subside. I can't look him in the eye.

At length he speaks in a tone that makes me feel like I'm three. "What did you do, Les?"

I feel the room fading. I'm about to pass out. Maybe I'm dying. I hear a voice that is, and yet isn't, my own. "I killed him."

Chapter 9

IN SAN FRANCISCO WE FINALLY FOUND A CITY that was big enough for the both of us. The years we spent there were the most harmonious of our lives. Addison did his thing and I did mine. As time wore on we did more and more things together. We finally seemed able to laugh at each other's peculiar ticks and eccentricities. Addison chased the guys on Castro and I dated no one. It was easier that way. When Addison was away I cherished my solitude. When he came back we laughed a lot and spent time with friends.

I didn't complain that Addison bounced from job to job, rarely keeping any of them for even a year. He didn't complain that I micromanaged our money, since I was paying for most everything. Addison probably knew I was going into debt to afford his lifestyle, but he never brought it up. I, too, looked the other way. My joy over the fact that I finally had a peaceful, stable relationship with my twin brother was worth too much to let money stand in the way.

Unfortunately, that meant we began neglecting more important things. Like visiting Mom, who lived in Portland, 750 miles to the north.

"She's in her 80's now, Addy. We can't take her for granted anymore."

"I know that, Bro," he said as he stood shirtless at the window checking out the passing guys on the street three stories below. "Why don't you fly her down here? That would be cheaper than both of us going up there."

"You know she's not well enough to travel alone," I reminded him.

"Naw. She only thinks she's not well. She'll probably outlive both of us," he said with a snort. "I mean, c'mon. What was it, forty years ago she quit smoking because the doctor said she only had a few years to live? Look at her now. Healthy as horse. It's just old age she can't stand. That's why she's always complaining. How many times has she said she's just waiting to die?" Addison whistled out the open window and waved at some guy walking by.

"Either way, it's pointless to argue," I said. "You know she's not going to do it. We're going to have to make a road trip real soon."

"If you say so, Bro. It's your dime." He shot me that goofy grin of his. "May as well be now though. I've got some applications in and may have another job soon."

"Yeah, I know. I've got to see if I can get some time off. Would next weekend work? Say, four days round-trip?"

"I guess so." He shrugged. "As long as we leave on Saturday. I've got a hot date with that bartender from The Edge on Friday night."

I rolled my eyes, but said nothing, even though I knew that meant he'd be asleep for the whole trip and I'd do all the driving. I had reconciled myself to being my brother's keeper for the rest of my life. I loved him too much to do otherwise.

Chapter 10

"MENTALLY FIT TO STAND TRIAL."

The lawyer's words are sinking in. I don't feel fit at all, mentally or otherwise. I've been grieving for days, ever since the memory of what I did came back. How could I have done such a thing? The question kept arising, but I avoided looking for the answer, for fear of what it might be.

"Trial?" I ask the lawyer. "What's the use? I'm already locked up. And I deserve it. Can't I just plead guilty and be done with it?"

"Just hold on, Les." (*Finally, someone gets my name right.*) "You've got to stop saying such things. It will only hurt your defense."

Bradley Frazer—tall, lanky, and dressed for a funeral—is cool as a cucumber. He seems unfazed by what I've done, though I am devastated by it. In fact, Frazer hasn't even brought it up. He's about ten years older than me and wears a wedding ring. He probably has kids at home, or maybe in college. What does his family think of him defending a murderer? Who would want to? He's got to be crooked.

"I'm indefensible!" I tell him.

"Now, just wait a minute," Frazer says, still in soothing tones. "I'm here to help you, Les. Let's not make any assumptions. Let's just get to know each other, OK?"

I give him a shrug, but can't meet his gaze.

The questions start. *Tell me your earliest memory. Describe your relationship with your parents. Who were your friends?* He sounds just like the shrink. And I give him all the same answers I gave Hunter. I've got nothing to hide now and nothing more to lose.

"Now tell me about Addison," Frazer says, probing the darker corners of my thoughts. "What is your earliest memory of him?"

This is a harder question. The grief hovers, held aloft only by the thin reeds of my refusal to think of my brother. It swoops toward me now as I try to form an answer.

Frazer hands me a box of Kleenex. "Take your time. I know this is hard, but it's important."

I dive in, heedless to the pain. I'm surprised at the twinge of happiness I feel just to call up memories of the good times we had together. I describe how inseparable Addison and I were throughout grade school. How Addison always played tricks on the other kids and then hid so that I got in trouble. It even makes me smile now to tell it.

Frazer probes deeper. "And how did your parents feel about Addison," he asks.

"Mom loved him, even more than me and Dad, I'm sure."

"Why do you think that is?"

"Probably because he was so much like her." I wince at my use of the past tense. I didn't mean to use it, but I guess my subconscious has accepted the awful truth by now.

"In what way?" Frazer coaxes.

"He had her sense of humor, for one. The two of them used to laugh hysterically at the silliest of things. Dad hated it."

"Do you know why that was?"

"Because Mom's eyes lit up when she was with Addison, in a way they never did for Dad. I don't think it was intentional. I mean, I'm sure she loved my father, but there was no spark in their relationship."

Saying this takes me back to a time I hadn't thought of in a long, long time. "It was the same with Dad and me."

"What do you mean?"

"There was a deadness between us. I don't know if it was me or him. Maybe it was both. I guess we were as much alike as Mom and Addison."

The questions continued for probably another hour or two. Frazer explored every corner of my time with Addison, quizzing me on how I felt during the periods of his absence. He asked me about everything but *that* day. The day we went to visit Mom in Portland.

Chapter 11

THE TWELVE-HOUR DRIVE TO PORTLAND was as I predicted. Addison hadn't come home until seven in the morning, just an hour before we were to leave. It was obvious he hadn't gotten much sleep. I could tell because he didn't bother to describe to me his sexual exploits of the previous night. Normally he would go into gruesome detail and giggle as I squirmed.

Instead, he slept for most of the drive. But something else was not characteristic. During the times that he was awake—meal and bathroom breaks, the thirty-minute stretch of body-slinging curves as the interstate hugged the shoreline of Shasta Lake between Redding and Dunsmuir—Addison was unusually surly. Even when I asked him about his date, he declined to talk about it, preferring to sit in silence until he drifted back to sleep.

Once I brought up Mom and tried to discuss how we could persuade her it was time to move into a "facility," where she would be safer.

"No way!" Addison snapped at me. There was a fire in his eyes that scared me. "We're not going to warehouse her!" His anger was palpable.

"But Addy," I said, "It's not like that anymore. They've got this 'graduated care' thing—"

"Drop it, Les! I'm warning you!"

Was he threatening me? I'd never seen him this angry with me before. Others, yes. But not me. Sure, we'd tussled as kids and caused a few scrapes and bruises, but it was always brotherly. We never intended actual harm. But this. This was different.

We got to Mom's just after eight. We were exhausted—especially Addison—and he was still in a foul mood. But Mom was a night owl and she was prepared to sit up well past midnight yakking. I wouldn't call it conversation really. She might ask a question here or there, but no sooner would we begin to answer it than she would return to telling us her story.

I can't really blame her. Having lived alone myself for many years, I know how it is not to have anyone to talk to for days on end. You save up all your mundane stories of daily life and unleash them on the first set of ears that sits still long enough to hear you. I listened politely to Mom's health report, about her bunions and bowels, her arthritis and atherosclerosis. I heard about her heart and her hemorrhoids.

Addison, normally the one to dominate the conversation when Mom was involved, just moped and played with the cat. More than once I thought Mom was going to say something about his aloofness. But she only gave him an occasional prolonged look tinged with a certain wistfulness. A resignation that she shouldn't delve into whatever was bothering him.

They had that understanding, almost as strong as Addy and I did. Although I think he had the ability to shut her out when he wanted to. He couldn't do that to me. He had to go far away to break our bond.

"Mom," I said tentatively, glancing at my brother, "tomorrow I'd like to talk about your plans for the future."

"I'm going to bed," Addison barked, jumping to his feet. The cat vanished under the couch. "I think we all should."

"Oh, son, please," Mom begged. "Don't do this. Not now."

Son? I was taken aback to hear Mom call him that. He had always been *Addy* to her. Only Dad used generic forms of address with his children. I watched Mom's wistfulness blossom into full-blown despair as she stared into Addy's eyes. She wasn't afraid, nor was she angry. She just looked tired and defeated.

"It's time, Mom," was all he said, and headed for the guest bedroom.

Chapter 12

I'M FEELING STRANGELY DETACHED for a man about to get a life sentence. It feels more like a theater in here than a courtroom. I'm just waiting for the curtain to rise.

But the only curtain, I know, is the one behind which Addison sits in my mind. Dead Addison. I'm finally ready to draw it back and look at what I've done. I've been in the "recovery room" for months now. And I have recovered my composure. Enough of it anyway that Bradley Frazer is willing to bring me out in public. He even thinks he can defend me.

At this point I find his insistence on my innocence charming, if misguided. We have met frequently over the months, and have become friends of sorts. He must see something redeeming in me—to defend me pro bono as he's doing—but I don't know what it could be. I'm dull, mercurial, and often morose. Always Les. Brad would have liked Addison much better.

We talk about Addison on almost every visit. Brad explores my good memories, never the bad ones. And we never ever discuss That Day. He tells me to remember it, though I should do it privately. All along I thought that was because he was afraid I'd break down if I talked about it. Only this morning did he tell me that he was going to put me on the witness stand to tell the story in my own words.

Is that why I'm feeling this detachment? Or is it simply relief that I'm finally able go there? That dark place I've been afraid of for so long. Brad tells me that if I do it this once, I'll never have to relive That Day again. He says that Doctor Hunter can give me something for that. Something to help me sleep. Something to ease the pain. Only there's no pain now. Just the void I've filled with the good memories that Brad has been pulling out of me week by week.

The trial begins. Case number 07012004-17C: The State of Oregon vs. Lester A. McCubbin. Murder in the second degree.

It is immensely boring. Nothing like on TV. There are no hot women in business attire, for one. And, with the exception of Brad, the legal eagles here are a lot older and plainer than the young studs on television. There are no icy stares and knowing nods passing between the prosecution's table and the defense. There are no stunning speeches or gasps from the sparse audience in the gallery. Just lots of motions and petitions and legalese that seem to take no notice of me, the man whose fate they are deciding. I'm beginning to imagine that maybe the trial itself is to be my punishment. To sit here every day for the rest of my life.

The judge asks me to stand. "Do you understand the charges against you?" I say that I do. He asks my lawyer, "How does your client wish to plead?"

"Not guilty."

I consider contradicting him. It would be so much easier. I killed my brother. I admit it. Why not just say so and accept my fate?

But I say nothing and the trial proceeds.

Eventually the prosecution calls its first witness. Henry Miller, the groundskeeper at the Springwater Mobile Estates. "Have you ever seen the defendant before," the prosecutor asks the witness.

"I have," Miller says with certainty.

"Did you see him on April 9 of this year?"

"I did."

"Please tell the court where you saw him."

"On Avenue G, in front of his mother's trailer."

The prosecutor confirms with the witness that the address and time of day are consistent with the "day in question."

"Was anybody else with him at the time you saw him?" the prosecutor continues.

"Nope," Miller says. "Just him." He shoots me a look of pure loathing. I stare impassively back, both because I feel nothing and because I think it will unnerve him. I note that this is very Addison-like of me, which makes me chuckle to myself. This, it seems, *does* unnerve Mr. Miller.

More witnesses are called. All of them establish what I could plainly have told the court in a fraction of the time: I was at my mother's home from 8:20 PM onward on the evening of April 9.

My lawyer cross-examines each witness. He doesn't badger them or bring them to tears like the TV lawyers. He asks them each only if they saw anyone else with me. Are they able to identify any other of my mother's children by sight? Are they aware of another of her sons, in particular one named Addison? All of them say they are not. All of them say they saw only me that night.

I think I get where the lawyer's going with this. He wants to suggest that no one can place me and Addison at the scene at the same time. But it's not going to work. I've already said Addison was with me. Besides, where else would he be? We drove up together. We were staying the night with Mom. Our things were there. The car was parked out front.

The circumstantial evidence alone can convict me. But it won't have to. I'm going to take the stand and tell the whole sordid tale.

Chapter 13

IT'S DAY THREE OF THE TRIAL. The prosecution has just called its star witness. The one who can place me at the scene of the crime, the details of which I can no longer remember. My lawyer leans over and tells me to remain calm, no matter what she may say. This is hardly necessary. I've barely registered a pulse since the trial started. I am resigned to my fate. I deserve nothing better. These proceedings are superfluous.

"Please state your name for the record," the prosecutor tells the dark-eyed beauty. Her long, straight black hair reminds me of the pictures of my mother as a teenager. This makes me sad for some reason.

"Maria Savva."

"And what is your profession?"

"I'm an EMT."

"That would be an emergency medical technician, is that right?"

"Yes."

"In the course of performing your duties, were you called to the home at 15770 SE Springwater Road, Space 57, at approximately 1:55 AM on the morning of April 10?"

"I was."

"Please tell the court the nature of the emergency to which you responded."

"A neighbor at the Springwater Mobile Estates had called 911, reporting that she had heard shouting—calls for help—and several loud noises—things breaking and such—coming from the home next door. She was afraid that her elderly neighbor might have sustained an injury."

The prosecutor interrupts the witness to verify that the neighbor in question is Mrs. Helle from unit 56, who has already testified. He then asks Ms. Savva to describe what she found when she entered my mother's home.

"The only light in the home came from a few nightlights in various rooms. I could see across the living room into the kitchen, where a man's legs, clad in blue jeans, were visible on the floor. He was not moving. I called out as I entered and got no response."

A chill courses through me, despite my earlier detachment. I know she is about to describe my dead brother. I thought I had dealt with this reality, but I realize now that it's going to be harder than I thought. This is probably why Brad has told me to stay calm. I take a deep breath and try to maintain as the witness continues.

"I crossed the living room and turned on the kitchen light. I was then able to see that the man sprawled on the floor had sustained a serious head injury. His head lay in a pool of blood approximately two and a half feet across. The upper half of his white shirt was also saturated in blood."

"Was this blood from an additional wound?"

"No. I couldn't tell at first, but upon inspection I could see that the shirt had simply wicked up the blood from the puddle on the floor."

"Was the man dead?"

"It appeared so at first, but no, he was breathing."

My stomach somersaults. Addison didn't die immediately? Even with all that blood? How long did he suffer? Had he been conscious? Did he know he was dying? I killed him, yes, but I didn't mean to. And I hadn't wanted him to suffer. My heart aches anew for my brother. I don't want to hear any more.

"Can we call a recess or something?" I whisper urgently to my lawyer. "A motion? An objection? Anything?"

"Shh," Brad says. "Remember, just stay with me on this. You'll get your chance to tell your side of the story soon."

The prosecutor continues. "What did you determine to be his condition at the time?" he asks Ms. Savva. "The extent of his injuries."

"He was conscious, although in a catatonic state. He was most certainly in shock—pupils enlarged, breathing shallow. He did not respond to my voice or my touch. His right foot was also bent at an unnatural angle with respect to the tibia. The latter had been fractured."

"And you tended immediately to the man's injuries?" the prosecutor asked.

"Yes. After I stanched the bleeding from his head, I put a splint on the fractured leg so that we could transport him."

"Where was your partner, Mr. Kirkpatrick, as you were performing these duties."

"He was in the bedroom across the hall, attempting to revive the second victim."

My breath catches. I have been so consumed with the anguishing details of Addison's condition that I have nearly forgotten…

"Can you please describe this victim?"

"It was a woman, approximately eighty years of age, about five-five, 160 pounds. She was lying in bed and had stopped breathing."

"Was Mr. Kirkpatrick able to revive her?"

"No. It was far too late. She had apparently been dead for more than an hour."

"Were you able to ascertain the identity of the deceased?"

"Yes. Her name was Sarah Jane McCubbin."

"Let the record indicate that the witness has identified the mother of the defendant," the prosecutor instructs the stenographer.

The tears are flowing again. I want to run from the room, but I am shackled about the ankles. And I have nowhere to run in any case. I can't escape this. It's inside of me again. The gaping void is opening, threatening to swallow me.

"And can you also identify the man who lay injured on the kitchen floor?" the prosecutor asks Ms. Savva.

"Yes. It was him."

She's pointing at me. I don't understand.

"Let the record show," the prosecutor intones in a dramatic and final fashion, "that the witness is indicating the defendant, Lester Addison McCubbin."

Chapter 14

IT'S BEEN AT LEAST AN HOUR since the judge declared a recess after I passed out. The flood of memories and visual images that rushed into the blanks spots in my brain was just too much. My mind still reels, every time I try to comprehend what I heard in the courtroom and try to reconcile it.

The EMT said that I was lying in a pool of blood on my mother's kitchen floor. But that can't be. It was Addison. I remember it clearly now. It's everything after that I can't remember. Until I woke up to the smell of pickled death, the hospital room, enveloped in the drug-induced thickness and amnesia. How long had I been there? How much had I missed or forgotten?

"Do you think you're ready to go back in there?" Brad is asking me. "It won't be much longer now."

"I don't want to hear any more. Can't I just go back to the hospital and sleep?"

"You're going to have to hear it sometime," Brad insists. "The sooner you do, the sooner you can get up there and tell the court what really happened."

"I'm still not sure that's a good idea." My head is throbbing. All I can think about is the hospital drugs that can make it all go away. The drugs my lawyer hasn't let me have all week, saying that I need to be "clear-headed" for the trial. My head is anything but clear, but he won't budge on that decision.

"You were the only one who was there, Les. If the jury is going to know the truth, it will have to come from you."

"But there are pieces still missing," I protest. "I'm not sure anymore. I mean, if I was the one the EMTs found bleeding, then where was Addison?" I don't share the balance of that thought: *If Addison wasn't dead on the floor where I saw him, then where is he now? But, no, he is dead. I'm sure of that. Why else would I be on trial unless they'd found his body?*

A sudden wave of comprehension sweeps through my consciousness. "Oh, shit." I look up at Brad. "This is about my mother, isn't it? They think I killed her, don't they?"

Brad sighs and looks away without answering. "C'mon," he says. "Let's get back in there and get through the next hour. Then you can go back to the room and rest."

"With drugs?" I ask, without real hope.

"When the trial is over." He grabs me gently, but firmly, by my left bicep and helps me to my feet. Against my better judgment, and with a new sense of despair, I shuffle toward the courtroom. Before we reach the defense table, I'm suddenly chuckling to myself. *Once again, I'm going to take the fall for Addison, even after he's dead.*

A homicide detective, Kenneth Robinson, from the Portland Police Bureau is testifying now. He's describing the police theory on how I sustained my injuries. It is surreal to me that someone who doesn't know me, who wasn't there, is telling me what happened, when I myself can't be sure.

"The damage to the walls and cabinetry, along with the broken dishware and scattered cat food and other debris, suggest some sort of struggle, that substantial flailing occurred near—and up against—the refrigerator," Robinson says with an authority I seriously question.

"Do you mean to say that a fight took place?" the prosecutor asks.

"Not necessarily. What I mean to say is, at a typical crime scene such as this, yes, this evidence of a struggle would suggest a fight. But in this instance, we don't have a second person. All the DNA—the blood, the tissue—and the prints belong to the defendant. There is nothing to suggest that he fought with anyone but himself."

How can this be? Surely Addison would have left as much of a mark as I did. I slammed him into that refrigerator myself, more than once.

"Let me make sure I understand this," the prosecutor says, now pacing before the witness stand. He gives a conspiratorial glance toward the jury box, as if to claim credit for what we all know already: I'm guilty. "You're saying that the defendant threw only himself about the kitchen, slamming his own head into the refrigerator?"

"That's right," Robinson confirms.

"And that only his blood was found at the scene?"

"Also right."

"And there was no other DNA found?"

"Well, none other than the deceased's," Robinson clarifies. "But that's to be expected, as it was her home."

"Is it possible, Detective, that Mrs. McCubbin caused these injuries to her son?"

"Absolutely not."

"And why is that?"

"Well, besides her advanced age and arthritic condition, which would have precluded her from having the strength necessary to inflict such injuries on a healthy male such as the defendant, the time of death makes it impossible. Forensic evidence places the time of death at least two hours before the defendant's injuries occurred."

Well, of course my mother didn't attack me! What an idiot.

They didn't need to hire a know-it-all cop to prove my mother was already dead. I could have told them that. But the detective is way off base in saying that I injured myself. Addison and I fought. A knock-down, drag-out, fight to the death. *His* death.

Chapter 15

I'M NERVOUS UP HERE. I shouldn't be, Brad says. I'm simply going to tell the truth. But I don't like the spotlight. I've never liked to be the center of attention. Now, Addison—he loved it. He'd say anything to anyone about anything, even if he was just making it up as he went. It didn't seem to matter—not to him, not to anyone else. It was always me who had to do all the explaining. This, I guess, will be no different.

"Mr. McCubbin," Brad says to me, as though we were strangers, "would you please describe the events of April 9 to the court, beginning with your departure from San Francisco that morning?"

I do as he asks, describing Addison's condition, his inability to help with the driving, though I omit the reasons for that. Even in death I want to protect him from embarrassment. I tell the court about my brother's uncharacteristically surly attitude and unwillingness to carry on a conversation.

"So, you arrived at your mother's home about 8:30 PM, is that right?"

"Around then, yeah."

"What happened then?"

"Me and Addison went inside and put our suitcase in the guest room."

"Where was your mother at this time?"

"She was napping in front of the TV in the living room. We woke her up when we came through the back door."

"Weren't her doors locked?"

"Yeah, but I know where she hides the key."

I continue to describe the evening—how we listened to Mom's health complaints and cat stories and commentary on the items on the 10-o'clock news. I explain how I tried to raise the issue of moving Mom to a graduated-care facility, and how Addison got angry.

"Was that the end of the conversation?" Brad asks.

"Pretty much. At least until we'd all said goodnight and gotten into bed."

"And then?" Brad probes.

"Well, once we were in the guest room with the door closed, where Mom couldn't hear, I tried again to persuade Addison it was the right thing to do."

"You mean putting your mother in a facility?"

"Yeah. But he just got angrier. He refused to talk about it. So we just turned out the light and went to sleep."

"Did you fall asleep right away?"

"I didn't. I never do, unless there are meds involved. Addison— nothing bothers...uh"—I catch myself—"*bothered* him. He always slept like a baby."

"Even when he was angry, as he was on that night?"

"Yeah. He always left the worrying to me."

"What's the next thing you remember about that night?"

I'm remembering bits and pieces of a nightmare I was having, trying to sort out the dream parts from the waking parts. I'm taking too long. Brad coaxes me to answer.

"I was having a bad dream. I woke up with my heart pounding in my ears. I was fighting the bedcovers and I was all sweaty."

"What time was this?"

"I don't know. The only clock in the room was the old wind-up kind and it didn't glow in the dark."

"Go on. What did you do then?"

"Well, when I realized that Addison wasn't there, I got up. I had to pee, so I went to the bathroom first. Then I went to look for him."

"Did you find him?"

"Yes." I'm starting to tremble now as I try to formulate the words to describe what happened next.

"Where was he?" Brad asks. His tone is softer now. He understands how hard this is for me.

"In...in Mom's room."

"What was he doing there?"

"At first I couldn't see clearly. There was a nightlight in the hall, but the bedroom was dark. My eyes hadn't adjusted." I take a deep breath before continuing. "He was standing beside the bed holding a bed pillow—the one from the other side of the bed. He was just looking at Mom as she slept." I hesitate again, screwing up my courage. The shaking keeps getting worse.

"Did he see you?"

"Yes. There was a fire in his eyes again. Like the brief flash I saw during the drive up. It scared me."

"Did you react?"

"Not at first. I was too scared. But when he saw me he moved so fast I hardly knew what was happening. He wrapped the pillow—" A sob forces itself out of me, but I push on. I have to get through this. Get it over with. "He wrapped the pillow over Mom's face and pressed down so hard she couldn't breathe."

I stop to wipe the tears on my sleeve. I can't look at the lawyer or the jury. I see only my lap and the inside of the witness box. Brad does not push me. He hands me a box of Kleenex, which I take, but don't use.

"She started to kick and thrash," I bawl. "It was awful."

"Didn't you try to intervene?" It sounds like a taunt and I start to get angry.

"I did! But, I...I was too slow. And he was too strong! I mean, he was way more athletic than me. I tried to stop him! I did!"

"So what happened next?"

"We wrestled with the pillow for what seemed like an eternity, but I couldn't tear it away from Mom's face until it was too late. Addison didn't let go until she'd stopped moving."

"Did you stay with your mother or try to revive her then? Did you call 911 or summon help?"

"No. I...I couldn't. I mean, I couldn't even look at her. I ran out of the room, into the kitchen. I was trying to breathe. It felt like I was suffocating too."

"And Addison?"

"He followed me. I yelled at him to go away, leave me alone for a minute so I could think what to do."

"Did he?"

"No! Don't you see? That's why we fought. He started calling me ugly names and saying I was weak and cowardly. He said I should thank him for doing what needed to be done. That it was better this way."

"How did you react to these taunts?"

"I screamed at him and...and shoved his head into the refrigerator!" I'm starting to hyperventilate, but I plow onward. They need to know what really happened. "But he fought back. We wrestled for a long time, banging into the walls and cabinets. Things were falling and breaking. All I could see was this evil in his eyes. I...I'd never seen him like that before." The sobs come so rapidly now I can't continue.

After a moment, Brad says, "Just one more question, Les." I don't look up at him. "How did the fight end?"

I take several deep breaths before answering. "I k...killed him! I took his head and banged it into the refrigerator again and again until my strength was gone. His body slid to the floor and stopped moving. I watched as the blood began to ooze out across the white linoleum."

My head is splitting now. It hurts to think, to speak.

"And...and...that's the last thing I remember."

Chapter 16

IT'S ONLY BEEN AN HOUR since I was first here on the witness stand. My lawyer persuaded the judge to grant a short recess for me to "collect" myself after what was a more painful testimony than I had expected. But he denied Brad's request to delay the cross-examination until tomorrow. Brad says it's because the judge didn't want to deny the jurors the chance to compare my earlier answers with the ones I'm about to give.

I don't feel ready to face cross-examination. My breath is still coming in short, shallow gulps, and my heart is beating too hard. I don't want to wade into that sea of emotion and confusion again so soon. But the trial goes on anyway.

"Mr. McCubbin," the prosecutor begins. "You have told the court that you fought in your mother's kitchen with a brother named Addison, is that right?"

"Yes."

"And you would have us believe that it is this same Addison who callously murdered your mother just minutes earlier, am I correct?"

"Yes."

"And that you attempted to prevent him from doing so."

I nod.

"A verbal response, if you please, Mr. McCubbin," the judge says to me.

"Yes, I tried to stop him, but it was too late."

"That's a very noble thing to do, Mr. McCubbin," the prosecutor says in a tone so patronizing I want to slug him. Like he knows what it's like to accidentally kill your own brother!

"But how is it that none of the witnesses who have testified in this courtroom ever saw your brother at your mother's home, on that day or any other?"

"I don't know."

"And Detective Robinson has told us that there was no DNA to suggest that this Addison was ever at the scene of the crime. Can you explain how that might be?"

"No." This is turning out just like all the other times in my life when my twin brother managed to escape punishment and leave me to answer for him. He always had a knack for disappearing at just the right moment. But I'm tired of this. I can't do it anymore. I wish he were here now. That just once he take responsibility for himself."

"In fact," the prosecutor drives on, "none of the neighbors who testified ever heard your mother speak of a son named Addison throughout the nearly twenty years she has lived at the Springwater Mobile Estates."

I stare blankly at the prosecutor, willing my mind to be elsewhere. But there is nowhere else but the Void, and I want to be there even less.

"Don't you find that a little odd, Mr. McCubbin?"

I shrug, then remember that I have to speak. "I don't know." I try to shut him out, to tell myself that he doesn't matter, that there are not scores of faces in this room all trained on me, hanging on my every answer. But it's not working.

"And you would have the court believe that this brother—whom you claim to have injured, and who left no trace of his bleeding self at the scene—simply disappeared after smothering your mother with a pillow and leaving you in a pool of blood on the kitchen floor?"

I snap. "I said I can't remember!" I shout at him, jumping to my feet as the blood rushes to my face. My head begins to throb again.

The gavel hits the bench. "The witness will remain seated!" the judge commands. Brad is already on his feet, throwing me a pleading look. "Counsel," the judge says to him, "you will see to it that your client restrains himself, or I will add a contempt charge."

"Yes, your honor," Brad replies.

I'm already seated again—my hands under my thighs, lest they strangle the bastard—when the judge turns back to me. "Are we ready to continue, Mr. McCubbin?"

"Yessir—I mean, your honor." I hang my head, not in shame, but to avoid having to see the shit-eating smirk on the prosecutor's pinched little face. He's already firing the next question.

"You can't remember," he says with a conspiratorial glance at the jury. "And yet you expect this court to believe your word over that of half a dozen other witnesses?"

"Yeah—no—*whatever*. I don't really care who they believe," I said, fighting the urge to lunge at him.

"Like you don't really care who murdered your mother?"

"Objection!" Brad yells, jumping to his feet. My blood is boiling, but with effort I continue to sit on my hands.

"Sustained," the judge says with a rap of the gavel. "The jury will disregard the last question." He casts a disapproving look at the prosecutor.

"I'm sorry, your honor," the prosecutor says in the same patronizing tone he's using with me, "it's just that I'm having a hard time understanding the aloofness of a man whose mother has just been murdered."

"Mr. Chiaravalle!" The gavel comes down again. "I'm warning you! One more such remark and it is you that I will hold in contempt." He again instructs the jury to disregard the prosecutor's remark.

The prosecutor is already heading back to his seat. "I have no more questions, your honor."

Chapter 17

THE TRIAL IS IN ITS FOURTH DAY NOW. Brad has convinced the judge to allow me to appear without shackles. He told the judge that my "agitated mental state" could be directly attributed to the claustrophobia produced by such confinement. Dr. Hunter has signed off on this diagnosis. The judge made Brad promise that he would keep me under control. Brad, in turn, has made me promise that I would behave.

Our LA and San Francisco landlords have both just finished testifying that they've never met Addison. Both said they rented apartments to only me. Like this is supposed to mean something? Of course they rented to me. Addison never met a bill he wouldn't skip out on. I paid for everything. Besides, he wouldn't have passed the employment check necessary to sign a lease.

I'm not really sure where Brad is going with this line of questioning. Is he trying to demonstrate that Addy has always been a master at going unnoticed? Attempting to explain how he could have gotten in and out of my mother's house undetected? Does he think that he can save me if no one can prove my brother was there? After all, they say there was no body. It might work, I guess. But if the jury believes that, then they'll think I killed Mom. I just have to trust Brad, I guess. I'm not a lawyer.

Brad calls the next witness: Carol Geisler. A name I haven't heard in twenty years. My first-grade teacher. I recognize her immediately, though she's in her sixties now, at least. Good memories begin to seep into my consciousness. Helping her grade papers after school, applying gold stars to the ones that merited them. Making copies for her in the school secretary's office. She glances my way as she takes the stand. She smiles wanly, with kind eyes. I smile back.

"Ms. Geisler," Brad says, "you are retired at present, is that right?"

"Yes."

"And from what profession did you retire?"

"Teaching," Ms. Geisler says. "I taught for 33 years at Russell Elementary in Nampa, Idaho."

"And what grade were you teaching in 1976?"

"First."

"And was the defendant a student in your class that year?"

"Yes."

"Was his twin brother Addison also in your class?"

"No." Ms. Geisler shakes her head. "No," she says again. "There was only Lester."

"How many first grade classes were there at Russell that year, Ms. Geisler?"

"There were two. Mine and Ms. Magee's"

"Is it possible that Lester's brother was in Ms. Magee's class?"

"No. I'm certain of that. I knew all the students. We often switched classes for activities such as art and music, so I got to know all of them."

"Did you ever meet a student named Addison McCubbin?"

Ms. Geisler glances at me for a moment, then back at the lawyer. She has a quizzical expression. "Well, not a real student, no," she says, hesitating as she speaks.

"Well what other kind of student is there, Ms. Geisler?" Brad asks with a smirk.

Laughter ripples through the gallery. The judge wields the gavel and raps it on the bench. "Order!" The snickers subside.

"What I mean," Ms. Geisler says, again glancing in my direction, "is that Lester, as a child, would speak of a brother named Addison, and I would go along, but...well, I didn't really think he had a twin."

Ms. Geisler disappoints me, despite the earlier fond memories.

I don't recognize the next witness, either by name or in person. Her name is Madeleine Tessier.

"Ms. Tessier," Brad begins, "prior to retiring, in what profession did you work?"

"I was a registered nurse for 45 years."

"And where were you working in 1970?"

"At Saint Alphonsus Hospital in Boise."

"And what was your specialty at the time?"

"I was a trained midwife. I assisted the doctors in OB/GYN, mostly with deliveries and post-natal care."

"Did you ever work with Dr. Elphège Alcime, during that time?"

"Yes. I assisted Dr. Alcime with hundreds of deliveries before he passed away."

"Do you remember how many sets of twins you assisted Dr. Alcime in delivering?"

"I do. There were only five."

"And how many of those pairs were males?"

"Just two."

"Was one of those pairs born to Sarah Jane McCubbin?"

"Yes."

"And do you remember the names that Mr. and Mrs. McCubbin gave to those boys?"

"I do," Ms. Tessier said with certainty. "Lester and Addison."

Finally! Someone who will end this madness! Someone who knew my brother, even if only in the moments after we were born. I'm liking this woman now. I'm feeling a bond with her already. We appear to be the only two people in the room with memories of Addison.

"How can you be certain of that, Ms. Tessier, if I may ask? After all, that was forty years ago."

"Because it was a difficult birth, and I've never forgotten it."

"Please," Brad says to her deferentially. "Describe for the court this difficult birth that has left such an impression on you."

"Well, it had been a perfectly orderly pregnancy, although the ultrasound showed a very rare anomaly."

"What kind of anomaly was that?"

"The twins were dizygotic—that is to say, fraternal—but it appeared that the blastocysts had fused."

"Can you put that in layman's terms, Ms. Tessier?"

"Yes. Normally, you see, fraternal twins will develop completely separately in the womb. They will have separate chorions and amniotic sacs, the inner and outer enclosures that protect the developing fetuses. In the case of the McCubbin twins, however, the chorion—the outer enclosure was shared. This is something you usually only see with identical twins."

"Does this mean then, that the babies were in the same amniotic fluid?"Brad asked.

"No. That's the inner enclosure, which can only be shared among identical twins. These babies each had their own amniotic sacs, but that's all that separated them. The thicker chorion wall surrounded both fetuses."

"Did this development complicate the pregnancy?"

"No, not in and of itself," Ms. Tessier said. "But it did complicate the delivery."

"How so?"

"Well, early in the eight month, both amniotic sacs ruptured simultaneously. The doctor suspected that some physical stress or trauma to the mother was the cause, but Mrs. McCubbin was insistent that no such thing had occurred."

"And what exactly did this rupture mean?"

"Just what you would expect," Ms. Tessier said. "The babies were on their way."

"How then, did the arrangement of the fetuses complicate the delivery?"

"Once the amniotic sacs were breached, you see, the fetuses were able to comingle. It was over an hour before Mrs. McCubbin reached the hospital. By the time we saw her, the delivery was already in jeopardy."

"Can you explain why this was so?"

"Normally, twins will deliver sequentially, within minutes of each other. But an ultrasound showed that the McCubbin babies had become interlocked face-to-face, as though in an embrace. It was impossible for them to pass through the birth canal this way, so Dr. Alcime began a C-section immediately."

"And what was the result?"

"The first baby was delivered successfully within minutes, but we discovered only after extracting him from the womb that he was not entirely free of his twin. One of his tiny little fists had closed around the second baby's umbilical cord, resulting in a prolapse. This must have occurred very shortly after the amniotic sacs ruptured."

"And why do you say that?"

"Because Addison was dead—stillborn. Little Lester had strangled his twin brother."

Chapter 18

I JUMP TO MY FEET. I try to speak out against the vicious lie. But the voice that suddenly fills the room is not mine.

"Heeeeeeere's Addy!"

I'm stunned. Simultaneously elated and horrified. I can't comprehend what is happening. Addison is on the defense table, screaming. Not in anger or fear, but some kind of wild-eyed mania. Where did he come from? He laughs like a madman and jumps off the table, charging the witness stand.

"Died in the womb, you say? Stillborn?" he cackles to the witness. "Well, take a good look!" He begins to rip off his clothes. Buttons fly as he pulls his shirt apart. Belt and T-shirt fly across the room. The bailiff charges him and takes a shoe to the chin. Addison's already away, leaping onto the prosecution table. "I'm alive and kickin'! He kicks his pants off as the lawyers duck and run. He shimmies out of his boxers and flies over the gallery railing into the aisle, clad only in his socks now, spinning and dancing as he goes. It's even making me dizzy.

Two additional bailiffs are already moving up the aisle from the opposite end to intercept him. He turns back, still without any obvious concern, and still shouting things such as, "This real enough for you?" and "You can touch my junk if you don't believe me!"Seeing the first bailiff blocking his retreat, Addison veers into the gallery seating, running across the laps of those not fast or fortunate enough to get out of his way. He's hollering like a banshee.

He's back over the railing now and charging the bench. "Why don't you rule on this, Your Honor!," he says, gesticulating to his crotch. He's airborne, about to leap onto the witness stand, when I see wires and foil flying through the air.

Aaaagh! Addison is screaming and spasming, and so am I. Somehow I've gotten tangled in the taser's projectiles along with my brother. My head hits the railing of the witness stand and everything goes black.

Epilogue

SIX WEEKS AFTER THE TRIAL the newspaper still lies on the table. I like to look at it. "Mistrial" reads the headline.

I should think so. The whole thing was a farce from the beginning. The lying witnesses. The contemptuous prosecutor. The sudden appearance of Addison, who I was certain had died at my own hands. It was an embarrassment to the judicial system. Trying me for the death of someone who was still very much alive.

It's no wonder the judge decided to make it up to me. He could have just apologized. But he went so far as to have me released from that horrific hospital the very next day, and the state is now putting me up— all expenses paid—at this condo in Salem.

I've got my own apartment, small but with all the amenities. There's round the clock concierge service, exercise rooms, basketball hoops and other recreational facilities in the yard, and a dining room that serves three free meals a day. It's got top-notch security, too. The place even came furnished with just about everything I could want.

I've made some new friends since I've been here, something that's always been hard for me in the past. Some of the neighbors here are a little strange, and more than a few of them like to keep to themselves. I can relate to that. But there are so many friendly people in the building, it's hard not to get to know some of them. There are social nights, bingo and other games. Movies are shown every evening and there's always something on TV in the lounge.

I can't say I don't miss San Francisco—the restaurants, the views, the smell of the salt air. But, hey, I don't have to work here. No rent, no bills to pay. I get full medical care too. They even deliver my meds to my apartment, twice a day. I couldn't ask for any better service. They've stopped at nothing to make up for what they put me through.

The greatest relief, however, is to discover that I didn't actually kill Addison. I can't describe how happy that makes me. I can live with myself again. Not that I don't still miss him. After his courtroom antics, he had to be locked up—hospitalized, just like they'd done to me for all those months. I mean, what else could they do? Not only did he admit to killing Mom, but his bizarre behavior proved that he'd gone completely off his rocker. I don't know where he got to after our fight that night, but he's different now. I miss the old Addison, but I'd really rather not have anything to do with the new one.

It's been the roughest year of my life, but in the end I can say that losing Addison has really been the best thing that's ever happened to me.

END

This novella is dedicated to my friends at Bestsellerbound.com, who have inspired me to pursue new ideas.

Made in the USA
Middletown, DE
25 May 2019